God Gave Us Two

by Lisa Tawn Bergren • art by Laura J. Bryant

WATERBROOK
PRESS

GOD GAVE US TWO

Scripture quotations are taken from *The Living Bible* copyright © 1971.
Used by permission of Tyndale House Publishers, Inc., Wheaton, Illinois 60189.
All rights reserved.

Hardcover ISBN 978-1-57856-507-8

Published in the United States by WaterBrook, an imprint of the Crown Publishing Group,
a division of Penguin Random House LLC, New York.

WATERBROOK® and its deer colophon are registered trademarks of Penguin Random House LLC.

Library of Congress Cataloging-in-Publication Data

Bergren, Lisa Tawn.
    God gave us two / by Lisa Tawn Bergren; art by Laura J. Bryant.   1st ed.
       p.cm.
    Summary: Little Cub has questions about the new baby that Mama is expecting, but she
learns that babies are gifts from God.
    ISBN 1-57856-507-3
    [1. Babies—Fiction. 2. Brothers and sisters—fiction. 3. Polar bears—Fiction. 4.
Bears—Fiction. 5. Christian life   Fiction.] I. Bryant, Laura J , ill II title

PZ7.B452233 Gn 2001
[E]—dc21

                                                                    2001045353

Printed in the United States of America
2020

19

Children are a gift from God; they are his reward.

PSALM 127:3

"Time to get up,
sleepyhead," Mama said
one bright Sunday
morning.

But Little Cub wasn't
quite ready to wake up.
"You can take your
new baby to church,"
she said with a yawn.

"New baby? He's still
in my tummy, but he'll
come along too. Now
up and at 'em, sugarplum.
It's soon time to go."

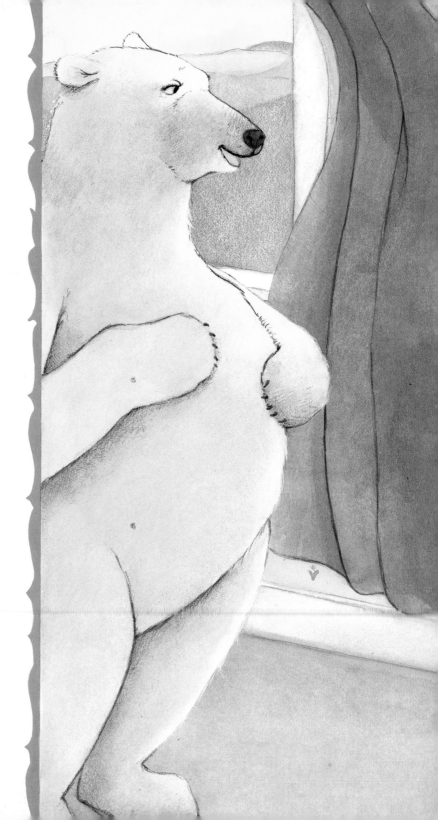

Little Cub yawned again and padded after her mother down
the hall to the bathroom. "Mama," she asked, "why do
you need a new baby?"

"We don't *need* a new baby, Little Cub," she said, nuzzling her
daughter's nose. "We *want* a new baby,
just like we wanted you. God gave us you.
Now he's given us two!"

Papa helped Little Cub dress for church. "Papa," she said, "if we don't like the new baby, can we send it back?"

"No, Little Cub. You don't send back a gift from God. He gave us you. Now he's given us two!"

On the way, Little Cub wondered aloud, "If the new baby cries too much, can I move next door?"

"Sorry, sweet pea," Mama said. "We want you with us until you're all grown up. Besides, you're going to like the new baby."

"Even when it cries?"

"Even when he cries."

"Little Cub," Papa said later, "do you realize how wonderful this is? You're going to be a big sister! The new baby will love you, just as we do."

"It will?" Little Cub asked.

"Oh yes," Papa and Mama both answered as one.

"You'll be able to play with the baby," Mama said, tickling her.

"And teach him how to say please and thank you and to burp with his mouth closed," Papa added.

 "You can have snowball fights together," Papa said, tossing a snowball in his hand.

"Or make snow angels together," Mama said, "when you don't feel like fighting."

"Will she go iceberg hoppin' and puffin pouncin' with me?"

"If she's anything like you, she will," Papa said.

"Or he," Mama reminded them, "if it's a baby brother."

Maybe being a big sister won't be all bad, Little Cub
thought. She would have someone to play with
who didn't hog the ball—like the seals did—and someone
who'd think she was smart and funny.
She wouldn't be the littlest bear anymore.
"Hmm," she whispered.
"God has given us two."

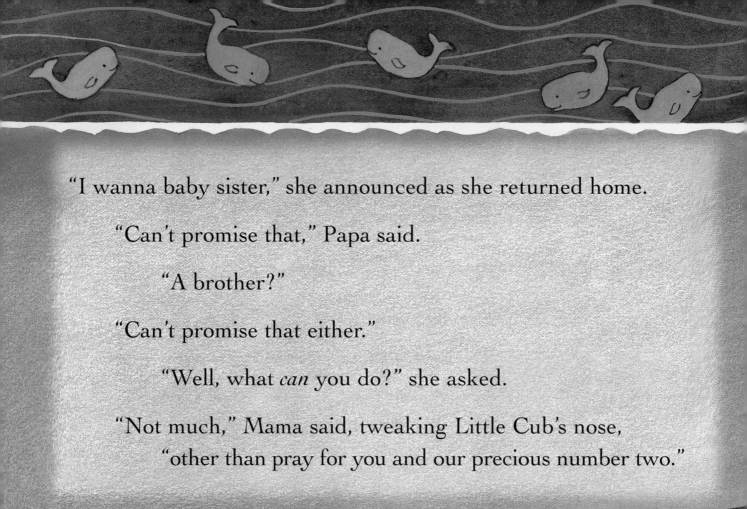

"I wanna baby sister," she announced as she returned home.

"Can't promise that," Papa said.

"A brother?"

"Can't promise that either."

"Well, what *can* you do?" she asked.

"Not much," Mama said, tweaking Little Cub's nose,
"other than pray for you and our precious number two."

That night, Little Cub tucked her doll into her
cradle and climbed up into bed to read
with Mama. It was becoming harder and harder
to find room on Mama's lap. Her lap was
getting smaller…

...and smaller...

…and smaller!

Her tummy was so big now that Little Cub
had to sit beside her.

"Ouch!" she said one night as they read her favorite story.

"What's wrong, Little Cub?"

"The baby poked me!"

Mama smiled wide. "Why, he's just moving about inside me,
like you did. He wants to remind us that he's there,
ready to come out any day." Mama squeezed Little Cub closer.
"God gave us you. And soon we'll meet number two!"

"Papa," Little Cub asked as they walked that night, "will the new baby look like me?"

"Maybe," Papa said. He held out his paw and caught some snow. "All these snowflakes are bright, white, and wet. But each one is different. Same Maker," he explained, looking up at the falling flakes, "but he's a creative Creator. We'll soon see, won't we?"

The next morning, Papa sent Carrie the caribou to fetch Little Cub's grandparents.

"It's time for me to take Mama to the hospital," he said. "You'll soon know if you have a baby sister or brother!"

"Papa," Little Cub said, "will you forget about me?"

"Never!" Papa said. "God gave us you. Now he's given us two!"

"No one will ever take your place," Mama said. "I promise. Now come out—I need a good-bye hug from my sweetest Little Cub."

Little Cub spent the day fishing with Grampa…

And baking cookies with Gramma…

Playing checkers with Grampa…

And hide-and-seek with the animals…

…until Papa came home.

"I have a surprise for you, Little Cub," he said.

"What?"

"You have a baby sister!"

"I do?"

"And a baby brother!"

"I do?"

"Yes, Little Cub, God gave us two!"

"No, Papa," Little Cub said proudly,
"God gave us three!"

Enjoy the rest of the God Gave Us series!

Available in eBook:

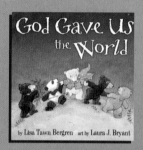

Coming January 2013

Available in Print:

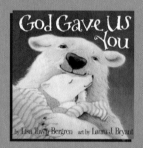

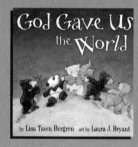

Coming January 2013

3-in-1 Treasury!

Available as Board Book: